PIRATES of the CARIBBEAN
JACK SPARROW

City of Gold

by Rob Kidd
Illustrated by Jean-Paul Orpinas

Based on the earlier life of the character, Jack Sparrow,
created for the theatrical motion picture,
Pirates of the Caribbean: The Curse of the Black Pearl
Screen story by Ted Elliott & Terry Rossio and Stuart Beattie and Jay Wolpert,
Screenplay by Ted Elliott & Terry Rossio,
and characters created for the theatrical motion pictures
Pirates of the Caribbean: Dead Man's Chest and
Pirates of the Caribbean: At World's End
written by Ted Elliott & Terry Rossio

Bath · New York · Singapore · Hong Kong

Special thanks to Ken Becker, Elizabeth Braswell
and Rich Thomas.

First published by Parragon in 2007
Parragon
Queen Street House
4 Queen Street
Bath BA1 1HE, UK

F. 435931
(student choice)

ISBN 978-1-4054-9998-9

Printed in Great Britain by Mackays of Chatham Ltd, Chatham Kent

City of Gold

CHAPTER ONE

A lone figure paced back and forth on a tiny patch of relatively solid land in the middle of a giant swamp. His red bandana was the only bright thing for miles. He was getting impatient, and sweat from the muggy heat was running down his face.

Gloom and greyness surrounded him like the muddy waters that obscured his feet. Big trees full of Spanish moss blocked most of the sunlight. The moss hung from the tree branches like hundreds of small intertwined snakes. Everything was moist. And itchy.

Flying insects – many probably carrying disease – swarmed above, forming buzzing grey clouds. Things dripped. Things oozed and bubbled. Things floated and bobbed in the murky depths.

The boy, one Jack Sparrow, was getting really tired of fending off all the vicious, man-eating creatures in these swamps. And – though you couldn't tell it from the permanent gloom here – the sun was setting. Shadows deepened and fireflies were beginning to dot the darkness under the trees. Jack just waited.

"What is taking her so long?" a bush whispered to him.

Jack rolled his eyes, wishing for once that he really *was* crazy, which was what everyone else believed.

Jack sighed dramatically and pushed aside some thick vines and marsh plants. Hidden behind the swampy flora was Fitzwilliam P. Dalton III, a sailor aboard Jack's boat, the mighty *Barnacle*. Fitzwilliam was from an aristocratic background and always looked the part. Even now, here in the swamp, his jacket looked spotless and his buckle shoes were well polished.

"Would you *be quiet*?" Jack shouted. Then, quickly realizing that he himself was being loud, he lowered his voice to a forced whisper. "There are certain ways to do things, you know. Hiding, for instance. Hiding, you might be surprised to learn, *often* requires not being seen or heard."

Jack moved the marsh plants back into place and adjusted leaves to hide Fitzwilliam.

"Jack Sparrow," came another voice, *behind* him this time.

The powerful mystic, Tia Dalma, parted the tall grass and emerged before Jack. There was no sign of a path, no sound of her approach. She had one hand on her hip and smiled eerily, showing her blue-white grin.

"How do you do that?" Jack demanded.

"Why did you call me here?" she asked, somewhat pointedly. "You know I prefer to stay deep in the wetlands."

"Well, there's a lot going on in my life," Jack answered airily, waving his hand. "Things I thought you should know about."

Tia Dalma opened her mouth to respond, but before she could, Jack had already launched into his story.

"See, it's like this," he began, "There's this amulet. It's called the Sun-and-Stars, savvy? So, this Sun-and-Stars was stolen from the village of a member of my crew named

Tumen. Lovely boy. My good crew and I – well, mostly *I*, but my good crew as well, recovered the amulet. But it does not end there. Not at all. In fact, it's just the beginning. We found this little bronze gem thing that we then inserted into this amulet, and after we did that, can you venture to guess what happened? No? Well, I will tell you. Everything the amulet touched turned into bronze. Yes, bronze. I know, I felt the same way about it. Who wants bronze? Apparently, someone. And that someone was named Madame Minuit – a beautiful pirate and – like you, Miss Dalma – a practitioner of the mystical arts. Not quite as good, I dare say. Although she does have these creepy snakes that emerge from her arms as if out of nowhere – you should look into getting yourself some. They might have them on clearance down at the mystics' market, or wherever it is you magic people get your goods. Anyway, we escaped from this New Orleanian lady by the skin of our teeth, and not long after we escaped, we bumped into – you will never believe this one – the mother of my first mate, Arabella. Now, why would you never believe this? Well, because the woman was supposed to have been dead as a crab cake. Turns out not only is she alive, but she is a pirate, sailing with another fellow we all thought dead – Left-Foot Louis. All this, *and* we're not even finished yet. There's also this weird chap sailing aboard her ship – Silverback. And the ship itself, the *Fleur de la Morte*, isn't all that normal – it disappears when the sails are unfurled. How do you find it, you might ask? With a special *compass* that *points* to said invisible ship! (I have to get me one of those.) This man Silverback had another gem – a silver one, and when that was put in the amulet, what do you think happened? I know, that's what I thought, too, but you're wrong! Everything that had turned bronze before was now turned into silver." Jack tapped his silver tooth and stared at Tia Dalma. Tia Dalma started to speak again, but Jack cut her off, continuing, "As if all that weren't enough, mummy dearest, Captain Smith of the *Fleur*, absconded with my first mate."*

Once more, Tia Dalma opened her mouth to speak.

"We think they're in New Orleans," Jack Sparrow said, cutting her off again.

Tia Dalma sneered at Jack, and he shivered.

"Okay, I'm done," he said nervously.

"You have come to me because you want to learn the way of the tide. Is that so, Jack Sparrow?"

*All this transpired in Vols. 5 and 6, *The Age of Bronze* and *Silver*

Jack wasn't surprised by her indirectness. "Come again?" he asked.

"This is what I hear from you." She waved a finger at him violently. "You want the final gold gem for the amulet. But you also want to be together with your lady, Arabella." She said this last piece with a little smile. Then she became stern. "You cannot have both, Jack Sparrow. Choose now."

Jack's mind raced. Before he could decide Tia Dalma shook her head and clicked her tongue. "You delay, Jack Sparrow." She stepped past him and parted the vines, revealing Fitzwilliam. "Perhaps *him* know the answer?" she said in her deep island accent.

Jack looked concerned. He should have known Tia Dalma would find Fitzwilliam. You don't get to be a powerful, mysterious practitioner of magic by missing the obvious.

Fitzwilliam was staring up at Tia Dalma with an embarrassed smile.

"We're here to rescue Miss Arabella Smith," the nobleman managed to spit out.

"Getting the final stone for the amulet would be nice, too," Jack quickly put in.

Tia Dalma sighed, looking at Jack sadly. "I can get you t' golden gem. But for the rest you are on your own. You will have to rescue your lady yourself."

Jack grinned. "That's hardly a problem there, love! 'Rescue' and 'recover' are my middle names!"

"You know I demand payment," the mystic said, rolling the words out luxuriously.

"Yes, yes, of course."

Jack began to dig around in his pockets. Surely he had *something*. Tia Dalma's tastes weren't always expensive – just weird.

"Uh," Jack stalled, patting his pockets

more desperately. There was nothing. Absolutely nothing. Not even a twig or a broken shell, things that would be right up Tia Dalma's alley.

"YOU!" Tia said, suddenly turning to Fitzwilliam and pointing.

The nobleman yelped and jumped back, causing the skiff he sat in to tip over and land him in the swamp.

"When you retrieve that which is lost to you," she continued, "that t'ing will be lost again. This time, to *me*."

"I beg your pardon?" Fitzwilliam asked, stuttering a little. "Could you be slightly more . . . specific?"

"Oh, shush," Jack said, waving his hands in Fitzwilliam's face. Then he turned to Tia Dalma. "Yes, yes, very well, we understand, we're clear to go and all. Will do . . . yes and, yes . . ."

"Very well, then." She leaned over and tapped Fitzwilliam's neck delicately. When she took her finger away, a deep black tattoo of something that looked very much like a crab remained.

"You will be marked until I have payment," she pronounced.

Jack stared at Fitzwilliam, eyes wide.

"What is it?" Fitzwilliam demanded, trying to keep calm, but clearly unnerved by Tia Dalma's touch.

"Nothing," Jack answered, a little too quickly.

The gloom seemed to gather around Tia Dalma. She wasn't moving exactly but was somehow still disappearing into the marsh as if the plants and water were slowly sucking her into them.

"You will find the last stone for your amulet, the golden one, at t' same place where your payment is. I will be looking forward to receiving it," she called to them, laughing as she disappeared.

"Fat lot of good that is," Jack said, scowling. "I thought she said she was going to 'get us t' golden gem', not 'confuse us with stupid riddles' and 'deliver idiotic messages'."

"What was that woman talking about?" Fitzwilliam demanded, turning on Jack. "About 'that which was lost to me' . . . and payment. Do you have *any* idea?"

"No," Jack said, shrugging. "No idea at all, mate." He turned the skiff over, hopped in and picked up an oar. Fitzwilliam, dripping with mud, joined him.

Fitzwilliam scowled, refusing to speak to Jack as the two rowed off into the bayou.

CHAPTER TWO

After poking around the maze of waterways that was the bayou, Jack and Fitzwilliam finally came out onto a canal. The trees opened up, and they had a clear view: New Orleans gleamed in the sunset. Literally. The entire city was silver!

Jack had accidentally turned it to bronze.* Then when Jack put the silver stone into the amulet, the city must have turned from bronze to silver!

*In Vol. 5, *The Age of Bronze*

"It looks like a city of the gods," Fitzwilliam said, moved by the sight.

The boys tied up the boat and stepped out into the city. The plan was to meet the rest of the crew at a hideout chosen by their crew mate Jean. It was perfect: the unused chapel of an old church, abandoned and overshadowed by a much bigger, newer church. The *Barnacle* itself was stowed a little upriver.

As they walked along the docks, Fitzwilliam looked around nervously.

"I hope that blasted harbourmaster does not bother us."

Jack frowned. Now that Fitzwilliam had mentioned it, it *was* surprising that they were being allowed to just choose anywhere they wanted to dock. He narrowed his eyes, looking around. There didn't seem to be the usual port police, harbour officials or gendarmes scurrying around. Strange.

And the people walking around seemed harried – or haunted. They kept their heads down as if they didn't want to be seen.

"Look!" Jack pointed.

Striding menacingly down the street was a pair of pirates, all in black. Tall, black boots, black bandoliers and black tricorn hats. They glared at everyone around them. People went out of their way to avoid them.

"What the deuce is going on here?" Jack wondered.

But Fitzwilliam wasn't listening. His attention was trained on a pawnshop. A glum-looking shopkeeper sat next to a barrel full of silver jewellery, dinnerware and goblets. Silver was literally cheaper than dirt in New Orleans now.

But what had attracted Fitzwilliam's attention was the *gold* jewellery in the window.

One pocket watch in particular. *His* pocket watch. The one that had been stolen from him by a crook on Isla Fortuna during the crew's quest for the Sword of Cortés.*

"We must go in here!" Fitzwilliam declared, grabbing Jack's shoulder and pulling him in. He made straight for his lost treasure.

"I love shopping as much as the next tourist," Jack said, "but shouldn't we get back to the others with–"

Jack stopped short. Another small gold object in a glass case grabbed his attention. It looked like a round gold pebble or stone. Or *gem*.

"The last stone!" Jack whispered, punching Fitzwilliam excitedly in the shoulder. "The gold one! There it is!"

"Oh, so it is," Fitzwilliam said, without taking his eyes off the watch. He couldn't

*For the full story, be sure to read Vol. 3, *The Pirate Chase*

17

tell if it had the inscription on the back . . .
If it did, it would *prove* it was his.

"Here's what we'll do, mate," Jack said,
rubbing his hands together while forming a
plan. "You distract the shop owner. *I'll* get
the gem."

"Jack," Fitzwilliam said disapprovingly,
"I'll not take part in your illegal little
ventures."

"It's *not* stealing," Jack said. The shopkeeper looked over at them, suspicious of
their low voices. Jack shot him a quick smile
and then pulled Fitzwilliam aside and whispered, "Look, *everyone* has been claiming
that this wretched amulet belongs to them –
Madame Minuit, Silverback, Tumen's
townsfolk . . . it can't belong to *everyone*.
Therefore, it must belong to no one.
Therefore, I'm not stealing it. Because no
one really owns it. Savvy?"

There was something wrong with this logic. Fitzwilliam was sure of it. But he needed that watch.

"Good sir," Fitzwilliam said in a grand, loud voice, turning to the shopkeeper. "How much for this here watch?"

"Oh, that's a beaut, ain't it?" the man said, brightening at the prospect of a real customer. "Nice Dutch craftsmanship. It will set y'all back a pretty penny. Though by the looks of it, y'all can easily afford such a thing."

Fitzwilliam was seething. *He* shouldn't have to pay for the watch – it was his to begin with!

"This?" he said, trying to sound indifferent. It was hard. "It looks like golden *junk* to me. I could be persuaded perhaps to take it off your hands . . ." Every word hurt.

As soon as he saw the nobleman and the

shopkeeper deeply involved with haggling over the watch, Jack set to work.

Not that he had a lot of experience taking things locked in glass cases – of course not. He had just picked up useful information here and there on his travels. Like how if you spat on your palms and pressed against the glass . . . like so . . . and up . . .

There was a little click as the pane of glass neatly popped out of its frame. Jack delicately lifted the gem from among the other charms, rings and trinkets. He rolled it in the palm of his hand. The last stone! They would finally unleash the full power of the amulet and maybe even solve the mystery of the City of Gold. The words of Tumen's grandfather came back to him: *Wherever the silver lives, the city is.*

Jack stuffed the gem in his pocket.

"Barely worth it, but thank you, good sir,"

Fitzwilliam said as he tipped a few coins out of his purse.

Fitzwilliam yanked the watch out of the man's hand. He turned it over. The inscription was still there: *To my little brother, with much love . . .* His eyes grew shiny as he thought of his long-lost sister who had given him the timepiece.

"Great, glad you got it, have to go," Jack said cheerfully, grabbing Fitzwilliam's arm and pulling him out the door.

"Jack, really!" the nobleman shouted.

"Never done this before, have you?" Jack asked, dramatically looking up and down the street and narrowing his eyes, searching for possible witnesses.

"*Stolen* things out of a perfectly reputable shop?" Fitzwilliam said sarcastically. "No, Jack, I must admit that is a life experience I have somehow *missed* up until this point."

21

"How reputable a shop could it be, dealing in stolen goods?" Jack pointed out, wisely.

"Okay, we'll quickly get back to the others, then come up with a plan to save Arabella," Jack said excitedly, leading Fitzwilliam down the street. "*Then* we'll see about Left-Foot Louis and Silverback. And then . . ."

But whatever Jack was about to say next was cut off. Another pair of the all-in-black Pirate Guards came striding ominously towards them. In fact, they were coming *straight* for them.

"How did they find out so quickly?" Jack wondered, feeling the gold stone in his pocket.

"Run?" Fitzwilliam asked.

"Run," Jack agreed.

CHAPTER THREE

Jack and Fitzwilliam turned and started sprinting down the narrow street. Fitzwilliam had, of course, trained with the best athletic instructors and kept his chest up, his shoulders back and his stride even. His buckle shoes clicked along the silver cobblestones. Jack just leaned back, flailed his arms and told his feet to go as fast as possible.

They rounded a corner, Jack grabbing the side of a building to keep himself steady as he skidded on the metal streets.

But just on the other side, they collided headfirst into another pair of Pirate Guards.

The one Jack slammed into was large, scarred, and had an official-looking medal pinned over his breast. Like a chief of police. He clapped a weighty club into his meaty fist.

"*Awright, then!*" the pirate said with breath that was worse than five-day-old cod. "Your papers, please!"

Jack and Fitzwilliam both blinked. They turned to look at each other.

"Beg pardon, mate?" Jack asked.

"Your papers." The pirate shook his club. "Hand over your papers, and we might let you be on your way, none the worse for wear."

"I'm sorry," Jack said. "But I'm new in town and my friend here – well, he's a few fish short of the daily catch, if you take my meaning . . ." Fitzwilliam glared at him. "And neither of us is really . . . certain . . . about what papers we're supposed to have."

"Don't you play Pass the Parcel with me, boys!" the pirate roared, shoving his face into theirs. Jack almost keeled over from the stench – something between stale rum and puke. The other pirates were grinning. "Yer travellers, ain't ye?"

"Well, yes . . ." Jack admitted.

"WELL, THEN, YE GOT TO HAVE YER TRAVELLER'S PAPERS!"

"No one told us about any papers when we disembarked!" Fitzwilliam shouted back, unable to stop himself. "What *is* this – a police state?"

Jack groaned and rolled his eyes. It was pretty bloody obvious that was *exactly* what it was – a bloody police state. With bloody pirates for a bloody police force.

"Oh, playing dumb with us, are ye?" the big pirate said, smiling nastily.

"Yes, it's a game he never seems to quite tire of," Jack said, interrupting. "Of course we have our traveller's papers . . . it's just that we were running a little errand – in that shop over there – buying stuff. For the girls, you know. Trinkets and things? Can't disappoint the ladies, can we?" He gave the pirate police officer a wink. "Anyway, we probably just left our papers there . . . so if you'll kindly let us . . . just . . . get them . . ."

He turned and casually tried to walk away. But he bumped into a pirate who was suddenly there. A solid, well-muscled pirate.

"Nice cannons ye got there," Jack said nervously, knocking on the man's huge and black-leather-covered biceps. He looked around – the six pirates made a tight ring around him and Fitzwilliam. There was no way to escape and no way they could fight off all of them. Even with his newly silver sword. He sighed and held his hands out.

"Take us away," he said sadly.

The two were marched down the streets of New Orleans with the six police behind them.

"This is all your fault, Jack!" Fitzwilliam hissed at him. "If you had not stolen that gold stone . . ."

"Do you never listen to pirates when they speak?" Jack whispered back. "This has nothing to do with that – OW!"

One of the Pirate Guards whacked Jack around the head with his club.

"No talkin' among the prisoners!" he growled.

They marched the rest of the way silently, Fitzwilliam fuming and Jack resisting the urge to rub his head. He was afraid he would be punished for that, too.

They were escorted upriver to a squat, Spanish-style fortification. It was made of such heavy stone that it appeared to be sinking into the marsh. There were bars on the windows and moss growing down its sides.

"I'm guessing this is our prison, then?" Jack asked, trying to sound cheerful.

"Nawwwww," the chief of the Pirate Guards said, not so cheerily. "*This* is just yer holding cell. Once they try ye and convict ye, they'll put you in the real prison. *Down river*. This is a fairy princess castle compared to *that*."

Jack and Fitzwilliam looked at each other.

They were pushed through the door and into the damp blackness beyond. There was a wide room where several Pirate Guards waited. At the far end was the entrance to a narrow hallway flanked by two guards.

"Lock 'em away," the chief of police said.

The boys were pushed down the narrow hallway, which had a number of cells running along its side. One of the barred doors was swung open and they were thrown in. Fitzwilliam was practically run headfirst into the back wall.

"We'll deal with you *later*," a pirate said. Grinning, he slammed the door shut, twisting the key with a flourish.

"Bit dramatic, don't you think?" Jack observed.

Sitting in the corner of the cell was an old sailor. He grinned up at Jack and toasted him with a brown glass bottle of something. It stank like turpentine.

"Drunk and disorderly, I'm guessing? How do," Jack said politely. "Pardon me, I just need to have a chat with my friend here."

He moved closer to Fitzwilliam.

"First I am an 'idiot', and now I am your

friend?" the nobleman asked drily. He waved his hand around the dank cell. "Look where you have landed us this time, 'Captain' Sparrow!"

"A jail. Placed here by pirates. *Pirates*. Not police or the *gendarme*. Pirates all dressed in black, *organized* like a police force. Or hadn't you noticed?" Jack leaned in, as if he were telling a great secret. "Since when, dear Fitzy, have you known pirates to be organized about *anything*? Or dressed in matching uniforms? They're not exactly known for their team spirit. Something very odd is going on in New Orleans."

"Apart from it being turned entirely into silver?" Fitzwilliam asked.

But Jack was already not paying attention. The chief of the Pirate Guards was calling his troops to order. Jack gestured to Fitzwilliam: they should be quiet and listen.

"Now, gents, Madame Minuit needs a detachment to help guard the mines . . ."

Jack and Fitzwilliam looked at each other. Madame Minuit? *Mines*?

"That witch is in complete control of the city now?" Jack asked.

"And since when does New Orleans have mines?" Fitzwilliam said.

"All right, you two stay and guard the prisoners," the chief announced. "The rest of you lot come with me."

The heavy tramping of many boots filed off into the distance.

"We've got to get out of here," Jack said.

CHAPTER FOUR

$\mathcal{J}$ack had been trying to pick the lock of the cell for at least an hour.

Fitzwilliam sat with his head in his hands. Even their old sailor cellmate looked disappointed.

"No, really, just a moment now. A trick I picked up in Singapore . . ." Jack said, trying to sound enthusiastic. Getting frustrated, he jammed the bent piece of metal extra hard into the keyhole. It broke with an amazingly loud snap. Both pieces flew outside the cell in opposite directions.

"Oh, bravo, Jack," Fitzwilliam said, clapping his hands. "Well done."

"I don't see *you* with any better ideas!" Jack pointed out, frowning at him.

"Nice doggy," said the old sailor.

Jack and Fitzwilliam turned to look.

Outside the cell, down the hall a little way, was indeed a sandy-coloured mutt. It looked more like a floor mat than a house pet, though its tail was bushy and its eyes were bright.

What caught Jack's attention, though, was the ring of keys dangling from its mouth, one of which looked as if it fitted the lock of their jail cell.

"Nice doggy," Jack repeated, getting down on his knees. Fitzwilliam followed suit.

The dog didn't budge. It tilted its head as

if it were trying to work out what Jack was asking for.

"*Come on*," Jack said, losing his patience. He stuck his hand through the bars and tried to gesture to the dog to come closer. "Come on, you mangy mutt . . ."

The dog cocked his head at him.

Jack looked around the cell for something to entice the dog with. But there were no bones, not even a stick lying around. Nothing.

Then an idea came to him.

Before Fitzwilliam could protest, Jack whipped the nobleman's beloved pocket watch out of its fob and dangled it outside the cell.

"Give that back to me now, Sparrow!" Fitzwilliam demanded.

"Shh," Jack said, not even turning back to look at his angry friend. "Here, doggy, look at this, eh? This is a *nice* toy, this is. All golden and sparkly . . ."

He bounced it and swung it enticingly. The dog's eyes followed its every move.

Jack took the watch and threw it out at him, holding the end of the chain and snapping it back at the last minute like a yo-yo.

"That is fine Dutch craftsmanship – not to mention great sentimental value – you are toying with!" Fitzwilliam raged.

The dog came forward a step, lifting a paw.

"Here we go, nice doggy." Jack flipped the watch out again.

This time the dog couldn't resist. He pounced.

Jack snapped the watch back into his right hand. With his left, he reached out and grabbed the keys.

The dog barked.

"Shut it up, Jack!" Fitzwilliam said,

panicked. But not too panicked to grab his precious watch back.

"Do I have to do *everything* around here?" Jack demanded.

"Arf, arf," the old man in the corner coughed obligingly.

"Aaaaaaaaaahhhhh, shut yer trap, ye old drunk," a Pirate Guard called out.

"*Thank* you," Jack said, pressing his hands together and giving a little bow. "At least *someone* else is pulling his weight around here."

Then he pushed his hands through the bars and set about unlocking their cell with the key. The latch clicked and the door swung open.

"Ah, the heady stench of freedom," Jack said, taking a sniff of the close, foul air. He and Fitzwilliam stepped out. "You coming?" he asked the old sailor.

"Nice doggy," he answered instead, patting the ground. The dog came bounding in, wagging its tail and panting. It sat next to the old man, who began to pet it.

"Huh," Jack said, narrowing his eyes. Then he lifted one foot dramatically to indicate their exit.

Jack and Fitzwilliam made their way quietly through the twilight city. Darkness had begun to pool in the streets and at corners . . . the street lamps had all turned into silver. A thin rain drizzled down, making everything greyer. Fortunately, it was easy to see the soaring silver steeple of the tallest church in the city and navigate by that.

It was completely dark by the time they made it to the church. Jack and Fitzwilliam went around to the back, through the churchyard. On the far side, past old graves and unpruned trees, was the much older-looking chapel. The two boys hurried down the steps, looking over their shoulders to see if they were being followed.

In the dank chapel, a cheery little fire crackled and the rest of Jack's crew – Jean, Tumen and Tim – sat around it. Constance, Jean's sister who had been turned into a cat, was stretched out luxuriously, cleaning her paws.

"We're back," Jack said dramatically.

"*Mon Dieu!*" Jean exclaimed, seeing the crab tattoo on Fitzwilliam. "What has happened to your *neck*?"

"It is . . . ah . . . a long story . . ." Fitzwilliam said, rubbing the place where Tia Dalma had touched him.

"It looks like black magic," Tumen said. "So you saw your strange friend, then, Jack?"

"Yes, but better than that. We found *this*."

Jack swung around an old chair with a tattered velvet seat and sat on it backwards. He pulled the gold gem out of his pocket. It gleamed in the firelight.

Tumen's black eyes went even darker with disappointment. The people of Tumen's village had warned against the use of the amulet and its power.

"I thought you said you were not interested in magical things any more, Jack," he said quietly.

"Yes . . . well . . ." Jack mumbled. "Aren't you the *least* bit curious about what it does?"

"No," Tumen said promptly. "Do not put it in the medallion, Jack. Remember what my grandfather said about the Sun-and-Stars medallion. It is very powerful . . . but also very dangerous."

"And, what about you three?" Fitzwilliam asked, changing the subject. "Have you had any luck finding Arabella or her mother?"

"Ah, no," Jean said quickly.

"There's been no sightings of the pirate queen," Tim added, tossing a pebble into the fire. "Or the *Fleur de la Morte*."

"She's probably kept it invisible. No point raising the alarm when you're on the run and trying to get the jump on two other notorious pirates," Jack said, a little grouchily. "And she's not really so much a pirate queen, as an annoying captain . . ."

"We *did* hear *un rumeur* about Left-Foot and Silverback," Jean added. "They have been seen with the higher-ups in the Pirate Guard police force."

"You fellas hear that?" Tim asked. He cocked his head to listen.

"Boots," Tumen said, frowning. "On the pavement outside."

"The police!" Jack said, leaping up. He shoved the golden stone back into his pocket.

"There is a window at the back," Jean said.

Tumen stamped out the fire. The five boys and Constance clambered over old statues and columns to the dark back of the chapel, where a small metal grate covered a window. Jack slipped his knife around the edge and neatly popped it out. They all crawled out into the deserted, overgrown back corner of the churchyard. It probably would have been quite pretty and peaceful in daylight, with its vines, wildflowers and leafy trees. But it was night, they were trying to run away from the bad guys and it was raining even harder than before. And the ten-foot ornate iron fence at the back with the spiky points was not so much *decorative* as it was a perfect obstacle to their escape.

"What do we do now, Jack?" Fitzwilliam whispered, and he wasn't being his usual sarcastic self. The police were closing in on the chapel. If they found the remains of the fire in there, they would know someone else was in the area . . .

Jack looked around. Rain poured down on his face, dragging the hair into his eyes. At least it was a little less wet under . . . "The trees!" he realized. "Everyone, up into the trees!"

Without questioning him, everyone immediately chose a tree and climbed up it.

They made it up just in time. The Pirate Guards were splashing through the puddles towards them, waving their torches around.

"'Tis nothing here, Cap'n," one of them said.

"Well, someone reported *some*thing. You lot smell smoke?" a familiar voice said.

Jack and Fitzwilliam looked at each other – it was the chief of police, the big guy who had first caught them and locked them up.

And then Fitzwilliam felt a sneeze coming on. The nobleman's eyes went wide with effort, and he pushed his finger under his nose, trying to stop it.

It didn't work.

The sneeze was extremely loud and extremely *un*gentlemanly, as though he had been saving it up for years. Fitzwilliam immediately slapped his hands over his mouth and nose, but it was too late.

"Here, now! What were that noise?" the police chief demanded, raising his torch up into the tree. The fire leaped and caught at some of the lower leaves. They hissed and sizzled in the heat of the flames. "There's somebody up there! Lefty, climb up that tree and see what's amiss!"

A Pirate Guard officer came over. He looked a little dubious about scaling the slick bark in the rain, but steeled himself and stepped a foot up . . .

At that moment, Constance came yowling out of the nearby tree. She staggered in front of the Pirate Guard, hissing and coughing. The rain had matted down her already disgusting hair. With her tail bristling and fur standing on end, she looked more like a monster than a cat.

"What in the Seven Seas is *that*?" the police chief gasped. Constance continued to cough and hack . . . finally throwing up a giant hairball, which landed an inch away from his boots.

"Yuck," said Lefty, somewhat uncharacteristically for a pirate. But, it really *was* disgusting.

"That'll put me off me grog for a fortnight," the chief said. "Well, I guess that's what the noise was – it's really rainin' cats and dogs, ain't it?" The police chief laughed.

The other Pirate Guard laughed along. It sounded *very* forced.

"Come on, lads," the chief said, "I've had enough of this business tonight. You lot go back to the station house. I've got to get my report on the state of the mines in to Madame Minuit. And the third division hasn't reported in yet!" His brow furrowed. "They'll be dancin' if I don't hear from them before I have to see her!"

The Pirate Guards scattered – probably to the closest tavern, if Jack knew pirates. Which he did. The Police Chief took one more long look around the churchyard. Then he gave a disgusted look at Constance, shook his head and strolled off.

The moment he was out of sight, Jack leaped to the ground, landing as if he had been falling out of trees his whole life.

"Quick, we've got to follow him!" he hissed.

Tumen, Jean and Tim leaped nimbly out of their hiding spots. Fitzwilliam landed elegantly.

"Good job, Constance!" Jean cooed, picking up the cat. "You saved us all!"

Jean gave Jack a look.

"All right, all right, good job," Jack said grudgingly. "The cat has made a contribution. Well done, et cetera. Now, we have to follow that Pirate Guard!"

"But why?" Jean asked, still scratching Constance under the neck. "How will *that* help us?"

"Because," Jack said patiently, "he is going to report to Madame Minuit. Besides all the various revenges some of us would like to take on Madame Minuit–" Tim nodded vigorously at this, "–she will *also* lead us to Silverback and Left-Foot Louis, and, as we know, that's where Arabella's fierce mummy is headed!"

The three other boys stood there blinking, not understanding the connection. Even Constance seemed confused.

Jack sighed. "How else would the Madame have known to go after our Tim Hawk here? Silverback somehow knew his family had the Silver Bullet and thought they might have some clue about the location of the amulet itself. And unless the entire Caribbean also somehow knows this, it would be an extremely strange coincidence indeed for *both* him *and* Madame Minuit to be interested in the amulet *and* our Tim Hawk, don't you think?

"Not to mention the fact that you've already said Silverback and Left-Foot Louis were seen with the Pirate Guard muckety-mucks. And when we find them, *chasing* Silverback and our old friend Left-Foot will be the irate Captain Laura Smith, wanting her revenge on the mutineers. And *with* Captain Smith will be her daughter and our first mate, Arabella. So in order to find and rescue our friend – Arabella, if you haven't been paying attention – we have to follow this police chief to Madame Minuit."

Jack looked each one of them in the eye. "Savvy?"

CHAPTER FIVE

Following the chief of the Pirate Guards, the crew of the *Barnacle* tiptoed around street corners, slunk in the darkest shadows and hid in convenient doorways. Avoiding New Orleans's new police cost them a lot of time and almost made them lose their target. Bad weather made it even more difficult. In the rain, the silver streets were far more slippery than stone ones. They passed a young woman also having trouble keeping her balance on high-heeled shoes while hurrying along, keeping her hood down in the rain. The chief of police touched his hat and smiled as he passed her.

Fitzwilliam also tipped his hat and Jean gave a little bow, but Jack just frowned.

"Where are your manners, Jack?" Fitzwilliam demanded as soon as the woman was out of sight.

"A better question would be: why didn't that big lug arrest her? Or demand her papers? There's a curfew, remember?"

No one had an answer, except Jean.

"Maybe it's all right for ladies, *non*?" he said innocently.

They pressed on . . . and came to a fork. In the rain and the darkness, it was impossible to see more than a dozen feet in front of them. The police chief could have gone down either of the two streets that lay before the crew.

"All right, we'll split up, then," Jack decided. "Whoever finds him first will send a runner back the other way. Just please, please, please try to watch your footing on this metal pavement. Now, Jean, Tumen, Tim – you take the left. Fitzy, you and I will go right."

"My name is Fitz*william*," the nobleman hissed.

"Oh, petty details, Fitzdalton . . ." Jack responded.

Jack and Fitzwilliam headed down a street that was little more than a back alley. Piles of rubbish overflowed into the street and a line of laundry hung low across the way, wet from the rain.

Suddenly, Jack shoved his arm across Fitzwilliam's chest and forced the nobleman back against a silver stone wall. Before the other boy could utter a protest, Jack put his finger up to his mouth to shush him. Then he pointed.

Just ahead, at the next street corner, were four Pirate Guards, changing shifts.

"How do we get past them?" Fitzwilliam asked. "The curfew . . ."

Jack looked around, eyeing some damp sheets hanging woefully from the closest clothes line.

"I have an idea . . ." he said.

*M*eanwhile, Jean, Tumen and Tim weren't having much better luck. They had only made it a little way before running into a pair of Pirate Guards. Worse, they were on a dead-end street with no doorways to escape through.

"Here! You lot! You got papers?" the pirate on the right bellowed. He was fat and held two pistols. His partner was whip-thin and looked mean. "It's after curfew, you know!"

The three boys looked at each other. There was no way they could take the two better-armed pirates in a straight fight.

"*Souple, eske ou pale kreyol?*" Jean asked, thinking quickly.

The two Pirate Guards looked at him blankly.

"You, there," the larger pirate gestured at Tumen. "What did he say?"

"*Matyox chawe. Xa majun Kär roma yiyawäj,*" the Mayan boy responded innocently.

The pirate rounded on Tim. "You look normal enough. Where are your papers?"

Tim gulped.

". . . *Ooomby,*" he finally said.

It was the first nonsense word that came into his head.

"*Ooomby goomby gamma do. Dooooo.*" He waved his hands around to show that he was seriously trying to tell them something.

All three sailors stared blankly at the guards.

"Bloody foreigners," the pirate said. He pushed his face into theirs and shouted, as if that would help them understand. "YOU NEED TO GET YOUR PAPERS. *PAPERS*? Lucky for you, I can't be bothered with mush-headed foreigners tonight. Just passed the chief – new orders. Be on your way, now, and don't let me catch you again!"

His partner just snarled.

The two pirates hobbled off into the rain.

"'Mush-headed foreigners'?" Tumen asked mildly. "I suppose their people came from *this* continent originally?"

"Did you hear that, about the chief?" Jean pointed out. "We've got to tell Jack; he's gone this way!"

"You stay here. I was the racing champion of Reading back in Britain. I'll be back sooner than you can make it to the end of this here alley," Tim said.

*M*eanwhile, down the other road, two oddly familiar – and rather ugly – ladies minced their way along, swathed from head to foot in soaking-wet pastel rain cloaks. Rain cloaks that looked suspiciously like sheets.

"This is never going to work, Jack," the one in pink said dejectedly.

"Just follow my lead, Fitzy," the other replied, pulling an improvised chartreuse hood down lower. There were now just two Pirate Guards at the street corner. Jack and Fitzwilliam tiptoed up to them, swaying their hips. Jack let out a high-pitched squeal of laughter.

"Good evening, boys," Jack said, batting his eyelashes at the guards.

"Evening, ma'am," a guard replied, tipping his hat.

"Awful night for a lass like you to be out, eh?" another guard said admiringly.

A little bit *too* admiringly.

"We're just on our way . . . to a, yes, a . . . *knitting* circle," Jack said, keeping his voice high and trying to step away. "You know the sort, where you crochet and afghanée, and, well, you know how it is, can't be late."

"Aw, just stay a few minutes," the policeman said. "Our shift gets so lonely . . ."

He waggled his eyebrows and made kissy lips. The situation was getting out of hand. Jack had no idea what to do.

Fortunately, Tim ran up just at that moment. He stopped, struck dumb at the weird scene before him.

"Oh, there you are, my boy," Jack said immediately, seeing an escape. "Naughty thing, running away from mamma like that!"

"Er . . . aye . . . bad me . . ." Tim said, his wide eyes shocked, more than a little freaked out.

"Come on then, lad, let's get you back home. There is a curfew, you know. Good night, officers! Keep up the good work!" Jack said in his high-pitched voice, waving his hand in the air delicately.

"Thank you, Timothy," Jack said in his normal voice. "You've just saved me from the terrible fate of becoming Mrs Big Ugly Police Guard."

"No worries," Tim said, still sizing Jack and Fitz up, even as they removed their makeshift ladies' clothing. What had he got himself into with this crew?

"Of all the humiliating . . ." Fitzwilliam shouted, pulling off and throwing aside the bright sheet he had been wearing.

"Actually, I thought you looked rather fetching," Jack said with a wink and a grin.

Tim filled the two boys in on the chief's whereabouts, and once they were reunited with Jean and Tumen, the five hurried to catch up to the police chief. He led them straight to a huge town hall. More Pirate Guards. There was no way the crew could march right in.

"Around the back," Jack suggested.

The rear of the building was definitely more promising. Although the door was locked, just under the roof was one window with its shutters open; someone had forgotten to close it against the rain. Leading up to it almost like a ladder was a thick growth of ivy on a trellis. In the blink of a mangy cat's eye, the five boys were scuttling up it.

Once inside the building, they found themselves in a small room off a long hall. At the far end was a narrow staircase. Sneaking down one flight they came out on a balcony that looked over the main ceremonial hall.

But it wasn't a ceremony that was taking place in the hall. Instead, it was where Madame Minuit had decided to set up shop.

She was wearing her stunning black-and-red dress and beautiful beaded hairnet. She sat in a fancy carved chair that seemed to be serving as a throne, flanked by half a dozen Pirate Guards. Before her was the chief of police, reporting in.

". . . mining is going quite well, Cap'n, I mean, *Madame*," he grinned, embarrassed.

She smiled benignly. Madame was

definitely pleased with his report. Obviously, Jack thought. If she *weren't* pleased, she would have had her pet snakes attack the man by now.

"Excellent," she said, smiling. "In only a few months the entire city shall be mined and shipped to Europe and the colonies. Good riddance!"

Jack and his friends all looked at each other. New Orleans *itself* was the mine!

"Madame Minuit, your next appointment is here," an attendant said softly, clicking his heels.

"Send them in," she responded carelessly, waving her hand like a queen.

Jack rolled his eyes and imitated her, waving his own hand.

Then Left-Foot Louis and Silverback entered the room, grinning like two very self-satisfied cats.

"It seems to be a summit of the vilest pirates in the Caribbean!" Fitzwilliam said in a whisper.

It looked bad, Jack had to agree. It was the five of them against the snake queen, the incredibly burly and scary police chief, the crystal-legged pirate-wizard, Silverback, and his friend, Left-Foot – who was basically a several-hundred-pound berserker.

The odds weren't good at all.

Jack leaned over the rail, scoping out the entire room and trying to come up with a plan for getting rid of all of the baddies at once.

The balustrade creaked loudly under his weight. Fitzwilliam and the others looked at him in horror. Part of the old wooden railing then broke off and landed right at Madame Minuit's feet.

Jack smiled weakly and waved.

CHAPTER SIX

Madame Minuit's mouth hung wide and slack with amazement.

The other pirates also looked up, their eyes murderous.

"*GET THEM!*" Madame Minuit screeched, finally finding her voice.

None of the pirates needed to be told twice.

"Run?" Fitzwilliam asked, by now used to their standard 'Plan B'.

"Run," Jack agreed, tired of the fact that this

was now their standard 'Plan B'. Someday, he wouldn't have to run from anyone. Someday he would have his own ship and sail the seas freely and not fear a single soul . . .

The five boys ran back the way they had come, up the stairs and down the hall to the office whose window they had climbed through. But a heavy wind must have blown in – the door to the office had banged shut and was now securely locked.

"What now?" Tumen asked, suspecting he knew the answer.

"Go down fighting?" Jack suggested bravely.

"Who's going down?" Jean demanded, grinning and drawing his sword. "Let's *get* these *mauvais types! Vive Nouvelle Orleans! Vive le Barnacle!*"

"Mates. Let's go, meet 'em head on!" Jack said, drawing his silver sword.

*E*veryone looked surprised when Jack and his friends burst through the double doors of the great hall.

"Come to meet your fate, *oui*?" Madame Minuit said, grinning with sparkling white teeth. "So be it. *Attack!*"

Left-Foot Louis, with a knife in each hand, made immediately for Jean and Tumen. He wasn't skilled the way Fitzwilliam was in two-handed fighting . . . but he was big. And fast. And strong. And joined by two other Pirate Guards.

Tumen took the left side of him, Jean the right. Constance paced this way and that, hissing and spitting as though she very much wanted to join the fight.

"*En garde!*" Jean shouted.

Meanwhile, Madame Minuit curled her hands like claws. Lightning flashed outside.

Her snakes began to appear, crawling down her arms from her back and neck.

"You escaped me once, you'll not escape me again!" she hissed at Tim.*

"I think we have a little disagreement on that point, ma'am," the boy taunted.

He threw his knife. It whistled through the air and buried itself right between the eyes of one of the snakes. Madame screeched and the serpent fell to the ground with a thump.

Another knife appeared in his hand, ready to throw. It was a little trick he had picked up in the dockyards of London and could now put to good use.

Madame Minuit pulled out a dagger of her own.

Tim smiled. He had been waiting for this fight for some time now.

*In Vol. 5, *The Age of Bronze*

Meanwhile, Jack and Fitzwilliam found themselves engaged in battle with the furious Pirate Guard police chief and four of his subordinates. Each had multiple weapons.

Jack looked around worriedly. His crew was fighting incredibly well, with new moves and skills they had picked up while adventuring with him. But they were still outnumbered and out-weaponed.

At least Jack's silver cutlass was holding up pretty well – but this was probably the one time in his life he would have preferred steel to precious metal – the steel would have been stronger.

Silverback was the only pirate not actively engaging anyone. He just stood in the rear, looking back and forth at each of the fights, as if trying to decide which one to join. His tooth and crystal leg were glowing faintly.

Before he could make a move, however, the door burst open. In rushed Captain Laura Smith with her first mate, Mr Reece . . . and Arabella! All had their swords drawn.

"*SILVERBACK!*" Captain Smith roared. "Ye villainous traitor!"

She charged at him, sword out and swinging.

Jack looked around, stunned. It was as if every pirate in the Caribbean were in the room.

Mr Reece engaged the Pirate Guard closest to him. Arabella picked another one at random and whacked him with the butt of his own musket.

Jack smiled. There was a pirate right behind him, ready to attack. The man came charging at Jack, who moved swiftly and casually out of the way, leaving the coast clear for the pirate to slam right into the adjoining wall.

Now at least, the battle was almost even. But not *easy*. Fitzwilliam had broken out into a sweat while fending off Pirate Guards. Jean had a gash on his right cheek and was slashing desperately at Left-Foot, but the giant pirate just kept coming and raining blows down on him. One of Madame Minuit's snakes was on the floor, not quite dead yet, and it still hissed and lunged at Tim's feet. Tim knew that if this snake bit him, its venom would make him a slave to Madame.

Arabella had to drop her musket – no time to load it. One of the Pirate Guards was running at her.

"Jack!" she shouted, looking for help.

"Good to see you!" Jack said, waving and smiling.

"Help!"

Jack pulled out a cutlass and blocked the guard's blow just in the nick of time.

Arabella ran to Jack and threw her arms around him.

"What say we all manage a little strategic retreat," Jack suggested. "We might actually live through this."

"Normally, I would say *fie on cowardice!*" Fitzwilliam said, parrying another blow from a Pirate Guard. "But we have Arabella back, and we have the amulet, so perhaps retreating would not equal a loss in this situation."

Arabella smiled.

"Crew!" Jack called out, "Proceed to the nearest exit!"

"Retreat?" Captain Smith bellowed, enraged. "*NEVER!*"

"He meant the crew of the *Barnacle*, mother," Arabella snapped. "Do ye ever listen?"

Arabella kicked a nearby opponent in the shin a little harder than she needed to, still angry with her mum. The pirate toppled like a bag of apples, rubbing his leg to ease the pain.

"This battle isn't going as well as I should like, either," Madame Minuit whispered to her police chief. "Perhaps we too should withdraw."

Slowly, one by one, Jean, Tumen, Tim, Arabella and Constance exited the building. Retreating in the opposite direction were their opponents: Pirate Guards, Left-Foot Louis and Silverback. Frustrated, Captain Smith stayed, looking for someone else to fight. Only Madam Minuit was left. Jack was protecting his crew's retreat by blocking Madame from the door, keeping her and her snakes a sword's length away.

"Who is this hussy?" Captain Smith demanded. "Is this the practitioner of magicks my Bell was telling me about?"

"I am no *hussy*!" Madame Minuit spat.

"Ooh, fight!" Jack said encouragingly.

But while Jack was distracted, one of Madame Minuit's snakes lashed out towards him, fangs glittering.

Jack yelped and leaped back.

Too late.

But instead of biting him, it hooked its fangs around the chain of the amulet – and pulled it from his neck.

Before Jack could do anything, another snake began to cough, vomiting up a perfectly round egg into Madame Minuit's hand.

She cackled evilly, smashing it to the ground. A cloud of foul-smelling smoke rose up and she disappeared into it, taking the amulet with her.

CHAPTER SEVEN

*O*utside, the rain had slowed to a drizzle. Jean, Tim, Fitzwilliam, Tumen and Arabella stood around wondering whether to pursue the bad guys who had fled or wait for Jack.

"Arabella, you look well," Fitzwilliam said a little stiffly, with a slight bow.

"So . . . do . . . ye," she answered, trying not to stare too hard at the black crab tattoo on his neck. "I like the, ah, artwork. Very modern-primitive."

"Ah, do not be so formal! Arabella, *mon*

cherie!" Jean cried, throwing his arms open and giving her a big hug. Arabella grinned. Fitzwilliam scowled. Tumen and Tim exchanged smiles. Constance spat. But not too much – and not actually *on* Arabella as she normally would.

Just then, the huge doors of city hall were pushed slowly, tiredly open. Creakily. Jack shuffled out, a little shamefaced, with Captain Smith and Mr Reece behind him.

"Where's Madame Minuit?" Arabella asked.

"Ah. Gone," Jack said wearily. He made a little motion with his hand. "One of her little . . . you know, the snakes . . . and the egg . . . and the poofing . . ."

"Bell!" Captain Smith said sharply. "What are you doing standing so close to that young man?"

The Captain shot a deadly look at Jean, who still had an arm around her daughter's waist.

"Mother!" Arabella said, putting her hands on her hips. "*STOP* telling me what to do!"

"Excuse me." Jack held up a finger. "Pardon me, excuse me, thank you, I really hate to interrupt you two . . . again. Bell, great having you back–"

"She's not 'back'," Captain Smith interrupted.

Jack ignored her.

". . . but maybe while the streets are full of priestesses, sages, giant angry pirates and Pirate Guards," he continued, "who all know where we are now, perhaps we should reconvene elsewhere?"

"Excellent idea," Mr Reece agreed. "I think the *Fleur de la Morte* would be the safest haven for all of us. And, ah, the largest one."

Jack couldn't really take offence at that. There was barely enough room on the

Barnacle for his crew . . . much less two more. Plus the *Fleur* was safer because of a special ability the ship had: when the sails were unfurled, the whole ship – and everyone on it – became invisible.

"So now, how *do* you find an invisible ship?" he asked curiously.

"With this." Captain Smith pulled a compass out of her pocket. It looked old and was made out of ebony with inlaid ivory on the case. Golden needles pointed to strange symbols on the dial, and a red fleur-de-lis definitely did not mark 'north'. She turned it around, clockwise and anticlockwise, until she was satisfied. "This way," she said, walking.

Jack couldn't help but be impressed. Captain of her own ship, fabulous hat, magical compass . . . Arabella's mum really did seem to have it all.

"I am so sick of this blasted city," Fitzwilliam shouted uncharacteristically, narrowly avoiding a muddy puddle. "I feel like we have been wandering around its wretched little streets for *weeks*."

"Looks like you won't have very much longer . . . look at that!" Captain Smith said, suddenly stopping.

"By Davy Jones's Locker . . ." Mr Reece said, stunned.

In the young night, a terrible scene unfolded before them.

Huge torches and lanterns were set burning in a ring in front of a block of buildings. Great bonfires flickered here and there for extra light. The infernal clanging of a hundred hammers and picks echoed through the night, as bare-chested men attacked the houses, breaking them into chunks. *Silver* chunks. Carts pulled by donkeys – and sometimes men – brought the piles over to low-riding barges tied to the pier, where they were dumped unceremoniously. Stalking through the fires and miners were pairs of Pirate Guards, making sure everyone was working and nothing was stolen.

"What are they doing?" Arabella said in horror.

"They're mining the city," Jack said grimly. "Just like Madame Minuit said. The entire thing. They're breaking up the city and selling it to Europe."

"Keep moving," Captain Smith said. "This looks like the worst place to be caught. Unless you all *want* to work in the mines."

She pointed – some of the workers had chains around their legs. Not exactly volunteers.

A few minutes later, the crew of the *Barnacle* – and the two remaining members of the *Fleur* – were performing the harrowing feat of stepping off a hidden embankment into what looked like thin air. But the moment each person set foot on the deck of the *Fleur de la Morte*, the whole ship came into view for them. It was a little disorienting.

"No more magic," Jack muttered to himself.

"Speaking of which, let us also speak of returning the amulet now?" Tumen said, as patiently as he could.

"Yes. About that." Jack paused, trying to think of some way to say it differently. ". . . it's gone."

"WHAT?" Tumen yelled desperately.

"Madame Minuit stole it. Right before she, you know," Jack made the little 'poofing' motion with his hands again.

"*You let her get the amulet again?!*" Tumen

screamed.

Jean put a hand on his friend's shoulder to calm him down. Tumen just closed his eyes and shook his head.

"I am *never* going to get to go home again," he said despairingly. "My village will never take me back as long as they think that I – or my friends – have stolen the amulet they were sworn to protect."

"Oh, stop it. We'll get it back," Jack said, his voice thick with emotion. "I just have to come up with a new plan, is all. . . ."

"I have an idea," Captain Smith said.

"Aye?" Jack asked. "Go on . . ."

"Let *me* approach Madame Minuit," she suggested. "I'll convince her that I'm double-crossing the lot of you. And to make it sound even more real, I'll ask for a cut of the profits . . ."

"Brilliant!" Jack said, clapping his hands

together. "I love all this double-crossing this one, triple-crossing that one. We'll have you get the amulet back . . ."

". . . *and* Left-Foot Louis and Silverback," Captain Smith finished, a murderous look on her face.

"Oh, yes. That, too," Jack said absently.

"What, did you think I would help you out of the goodness of my heart?" Arabella's mother asked Jack with a wry smile, seeing the look on his face.

"No, I think we are all fairly certain that you do not have a heart, much less any good in it," Jack answered.

"Thank you," Captain Smith said, smiling.

Arabella rolled her eyes and huffed.

"Well, this is indeed an *excellent* plan," Jack said, quickly putting himself between the two women before they could begin fighting again. "But Madame Minuit would never go for it. The benefits are too low for the stakes. Why should she trust you?"

"Ah, that's where you come in, Captain Sparrow," Laura said with a wink.

Jack put his hand to his chest and looked around him. "*Moi?*"

"Yes, *you*, Jack. You will pretend to be my prisoner. I will make it seem as though my plan – all along – was to double-cross you, to sweeten my deal with her."

Jack cocked an eyebrow. Then he resigned himself to the task.

"Sure," he said, "why not?"

CHAPTER EIGHT

Captain Laura Smith made her way through the streets of New Orleans as if she owned them.

"We spent the better part of our time here ducking around, avoiding people," Jack muttered. His hands were bound in front of him, and he was being marched behind Captain Smith and in front of Mr Reece.

They passed a group of Pirate Guards. Captain Smith saluted them, and they all touched their hats back. Almost reverently.

They seemed enthralled by the pirate queen, her flashing eyes and auburn hair.

"How does *she* get away with it?" Jack continued to grumble.

Mr Reece gave a dry chuckle. "Take a look at her. It's just who she is."

Arabella shook her head. She didn't have quite the Captain's presence or air of command, but she strode with the same gait and tossed her own hair the same way.

They managed to make it all the way to the city hall without being stopped or harassed.

Captain Smith threw open the huge silver doors of the town hall with great drama. Arabella rolled her eyes. The building was completely empty. The four strode through the entryway and into the grand hall. Again, there was no one. Just the lonely sound of their own footsteps on the creaking silver floorboards.

Captain Smith called out. "I'm here to see the famous Madame Minuit. Witch, show yourself!"

"Now, I would have gone with something a little more, well, I don't know, *polite*," Jack commented.

"The 'prisoner' has a point, Mum," Arabella said nervously.

There was a strange noise coming from the shadows, dry and whispery, like a ghost.

But the actual cause of the noise was far worse.

A horrifyingly gigantic snake came out of the gloom, making its way slowly and deliberately towards them. It was green and black with shiny, plate-like scales, huge white fangs and slitted eyes.

Captain Smith stood her ground, trying not to look nervous.

Arabella and Mr Reece didn't do quite as well.

Jack just sighed. As he had expected, there was a flash of light and a puff of smoke. Suddenly, in place of the snake stood Madame Minuit, in her pretty form.

"So bloody dramatic," Jack muttered. Mr Reece kicked him in the shin.

Captain Smith didn't even blink.

"Madame Minuit, I presume," Captain Smith said, with a curt little bow.

"Yes, *le* 'witch' you referred to before," the snake queen said languidly, in her thick French accent. "Why are you back here, Lady Pirate? You are as good as dead for attacking my compatriots."

"I was not fully aware of the details of the situation at the time," Captain Smith said, trying to sound contrite. "My only thoughts were for revenge – on Left-Foot Louis and

Silverback. They plotted a mutiny against me.* Forgive my earlier indiscretion. I have returned with a business opportunity that will benefit us both."

"I see. Go on." It was obvious from the tone of her voice that Madame Minuit didn't think Captain Smith had anything to offer her. In fact, from the look on her face it was clear she didn't care for the Captain of the *Fleur* – *at all*.

"I am a well-known smuggler on the Seven Seas – I have liaisons and connections everywhere from the Orient to the Outer Hebrides. I can help you move your silver anywhere in the world. All I ask is a share of the profits . . . and that Left-Foot and Silverback be handed over to me."

Madame Minuit just stared at her with un-blinking eyes, like a snake. She didn't say a word.

*In our previous volume, *Silver*

87

"Here, I have even brought you a gift of my good will," Captain Smith continued. Mr Reece pushed Jack forward. "Captain Jack Sparrow, biggest troublemaker on the Seven Seas. I know he's been a thorn in your side."

Madame Minuit laughed softly. "*Merci –* thank you. It is a lovely gesture. But why on earth would I need a *partner* when I can have all the gold for myself?"

"Because I . . . what?" Captain Smith stopped, suddenly realizing what the Madame had said. "*Gold?*"

"Gold?" Jack echoed. Mr Reece, also confused, didn't bother to shut him up this time.

Quick as lightning, a serpent shot out from Madame Minuit's wrist. It lunged not at the Captain, but at *Jack*. More specifically, Jack's *pocket*, the one where he kept the gold gem. Before he could react, it sprang back out of his pocket, the shiny orb in its mouth.

It dropped to the floor and slithered back over to Madame Minuit.

"What is the meaning of this?" Captain Smith demanded.

But Madame Minuit ignored the Captain. She pulled the Sun-and-Stars amulet out of her dress and triumphantly placed the gold gem in the final socket.

This was not going according to plan.

"No!" Arabella cried. Thinking faster than anyone else, she cut the one loose rope that was tying Jack's wrists together.

He was a little distracted; his tooth, the silver one, was tingling unpleasantly, as if he had just bitten into something very cold or sweet.

But he pulled himself together and leaped at Madame Minuit. He brought his fist down on the amulet, knocking it out of her hand. It smashed to the floor, the bronze, silver and gold gems popping out and rolling across the floor.

Madame Minuit let out a screech.

"Jack, look!" Arabella said, pointing to the floor.

Colour was creeping back into the world.

Everything that was silver was returning to its original state. The floorboards slowly became brown and softer looking, and brown shine licked up the banister like a flame. Out of the window, it looked as though a tin of paint had been poured over the entire city, filling it with colour and texture. Greens and blacks and blues and yellows broke forth as leaves and grass and stone and lamps all transformed into their normal states.

Arabella grabbed Jack's face and turned it towards her.

For a very scary moment, he thought she was going to kiss him.

But she was only looking at his tooth.

"Yer tooth! It's . . . gold," she said, a little surprised. "I suppose it was turned to gold before the gems fell out of the amulet – and stayed that way!"

"And . . . my sword!" Jack cried happily, pulling his rusty, then bronze, then silver cutlass out. But only the tip was gold. The rest was back to being its rusty old cruddy self. Jack almost threw it down to the ground in disgust.

Madame Minuit had stopped shrieking in rage. Her sudden silence was alarming.

She was *green* with anger, the whites of her eyes going red. Her hands were clawed and her back was arched.

Even the normally unflappable Captain Smith looked a little daunted. She moved closer to Arabella, standing between her and the snake queen.

"*Mes fils!*" Madame Minuit growled. "Come!"

The inner doors flew open and Left-Foot Louis and Silverback came rushing in, swords drawn.

"Here we go again," Jack said, reaching for his sword.

But before the two pirates could do anything, Madame Minuit attacked *them*!

Jack's jaw dropped in surprise as snakes launched from her fingertips and flew through the air. They landed on Silverback's and Left-Foot's necks and bit down, the snakes' bodies writhing as the poison pumped through their fangs.

The two pirates were instantly frozen, horror and amazement on their faces. They swayed a little, trying to break free – but they were paralyzed.

Madame Minuit quickly stepped between the two pirates, taking their hands in her own.

"*Sssslayen sseeereeess s'ynloth eressshi!*" she hissed in some horrible, ancient language. Her eyes rolled until only the whites showed – and then they turned scarlet, dripping blood.

"Ah . . ." Jack said. "Maybe we should . . ."

Silverback's crystal leg began to pulse in a thousand different colours. Tiny lights and shadows were thrown all over the room in a hypnotizing display.

Suddenly Madame Minuit threw back her head and let out a howl. It was an unearthly, horrible sound. Everyone – except for Left-Foot Louis and Silverback, who were unable – clapped their hands over their ears.

The outlines of Madame Minuit and the two pirates began to blur. Their skin grew soft, and it flowed in a sickly fashion. Their bodies melted and merged, falling to the floor in one pulsing, fleshy lump. Mr Reece looked away, feeling sick.

There was a blinding flash of green light.

Jack blinked. When he could see again, he wished he couldn't.

The thing rose up from the ground, now complete in its transformation. Madame Minuit, Silverback and Left-Foot Louis were gone. In their place was a giant serpent with three heads.

It threw its heads back and screamed.

"Get out of here, Bell," Jack ordered, drawing his sword and facing the dragon.

"Not on yer life, Captain Sparrow!" Arabella cried indignantly. "When have ye ever known me to desert, eh?"

"Bell, I mean it," Jack said firmly.

Arabella stood for a moment, stunned by Jack's sincerity. Finally, she nodded and saluted Jack.

"I'll take care of the ship until ye return, Captain," she promised.

"*If* I return," Jack said with a grim smile.

"You too, Laura," Mr Reece said, standing between her and the dragon.

"What are you talking about?" Captain Smith demanded. "And calling me by my first name! You chauvinistic . . ."

"Please. For me," Mr Reece said bravely. "I failed you during the mutiny;* let me make it up to you. I couldn't live with myself otherwise!"

Laura hesitated. So did her daughter.

"GO!" Jack and Reece shouted at the same time.

So they did.

"Well, that's that, then," Jack said bravely, turning to face the dragon. He and Mr Reece exchanged a grin, "As my friend Jean would say . . . *en garde!*"

* In Vol. 6, *Silver*

CHAPTER NINE

$\mathcal{T}$he beast hissed and drooled. The head that had once been Left-Foot's was now only vaguely recognizable, distorted with scales and large, pitted nostrils. It lunged back and forth on its disgustingly skinny neck, as if deciding where to attack first. Finally, it lashed out at Mr Reece.

The *Fleur*'s first mate brought up his rapier smartly and parried. Metal clanged on the giant yellow fangs, throwing sparks into the air.

But while he was distracted by Left-Foot,

he missed Silverback's attack. The sneaky pirate's head slithered along the ground on its own snakelike neck. It bit down hard on his leg.

"Oh. Oh, no. You *can't* be *serious*," Jack groaned, when Mr Reece went down with a cry. Gleaming drops of venom oozed out of twin nasty, bloody wounds.

"Why is it always me?" the Captain of the *Barnacle* continued to grumble, placing himself in between the serpent and his fallen companion.

The Madame Minuit snakehead hissed and pulled back, preparing to attack.

Jack stood without moving as the giant open mouth screamed down at him. At the very last second, he jumped out of the way. At the same time – and without looking – he brought his sword down behind him, where the Silverback snakehead was once again trying to sneak in and bite while Jack was distracted.

His sword hadn't cut very deeply. The soft gold tip of Jack's cutlass bent and skittered across the hard scaly plates, only gouging the flesh a little, but enough to hurt. The snakehead roared with anger and pain.

"Throw me your sword!" Jack called out to Reece.

Trying not to moan with pain, Mr Reece valiantly tossed Jack his shiny steel rapier. Jack caught it and spun, just in time to fend off another attack from the Left-Foot Louis snakehead.

Bringing the rapier out swiftly across his chest, Jack managed to sink the blade deep into the thing's neck.

Recovering quickly, the beast's Silverback snakehead once again slithered along the floor, aiming for Mr Reece.

"Watch it, mate!" Jack cried.

But the first mate of the *Fleur de la Morte* was barely conscious. He had one hand on his wound, trying to staunch the bleeding, and one hand with a dagger in it . . . which probably wouldn't have done much good.

Jack ran and leaped. He grabbed the chandelier and swung from it. With one swipe of his sword he cut the lamp's chain, then ran clear as the chandelier fell with a crash to the floor – and onto the Silverback snakehead's neck, preventing its open mouth from biting Mr Reece.

The beast was now even more enraged. Sparks glittered around its evil golden eyes. Lightning fast, it snapped at Jack.

Instead of trying to bite him, as Jack had expected, the beast whipped one of its long necks around his back and legs and pulled, crashing him to the ground.

The beast slithered out from under the fallen chandelier.

The main snakehead – the one formerly belonging to Madame Minuit – paused as Jack hesitated. Its gaze was terrifying.

Jack heard a voice but could not tell if it was coming from the snakehead, his own mind or somewhere else entirely.

"Jack Sssparrow?" the voice whispered. *"Everywhere you go, you bring chaosss and trouble. Violence and cursesss follow you like twin dogs . . . and your friends often have to bear the brunt of it. YOU turned this city silver. All because of the amulet . . . which you promised your little friend you would return to him. You didn't need to go looking for the gold gem, did you? Oh, but then you were curious . . . the power drew you in."*

Jack paused. Was that right? Was he totally blinded by the lure of the Sun-and-Stars amulet and the freedom it would provide him? He really didn't *need* to find the gold gem. Or the silver one, for that matter. They were just supposed to find the amulet and bring it back to Tumen's village.

He levelled his sword at the beast. It seemed fiercer than ever, and as it opened its jaws, Jack thought he'd be swallowed whole. He lifted his sword, closed his eyes and hoped for the best.

CHAPTER TEN

Outside the town hall, the crew of the *Barnacle* met up with Captain Smith and Arabella. Dawn was breaking over the newly un-silvered city. The crew stood in awe of what a beautiful city it was. None of them had really appreciated it before. But because the city had almost been lost, it felt especially sweet to have it back now – the iron balconies, the smell of damp cobble-stones down by the river, the flickering of rusty old streetlamps.

But they did not have much time to think about the resurrected city filled again with normalcy and, above all, hope. Clangs and crashes could be heard from inside the town hall.

"A beast, you say?" Fitzwilliam asked, attempting to sound more curious than worried.

"Of a sort," Arabella said, also trying to sound calm.

A window exploded outwards, shattering into a thousand bright pink pieces under the dawning sun.

Captain Smith flinched.

"I should be in there," she said, her hand going to her sword and hovering there, as if she were unable to decide whether or not to draw it.

"Aye, and me as well," Arabella said. The mother and daughter looked at each other for a long moment almost hopelessly.

Then a bloodcurdling, terrible scream filled the air. And everything went suddenly silent.

Fitzwilliam and Jean exchanged nervous looks.

"I'm going in," Arabella decided. Her mother was right behind her.

But before they could approach the building, the doors flew open. Out staggered Jack. His stomach was bleeding and there were gashes and black burns on his face. He was half dragging, half supporting Mr Reece, who was pale and unconscious.

"Miss me?" Jack said, exhausted, lowering Mr Reece down to the ground. Arabella tried to push past him to look inside, but Jack stopped her. "You don't want to see what's in there, lass. Most of that 'thing' disappeared in a blast of smoke. What remains smells like a steak that's much too well done. If you follow . . ."

Arabella made a disgusted face as she caught a whiff from inside the hall, and she proceeded no further.

"Mr Reece," Captain Smith said worriedly, kneeling down and looking at his wound.

"I'll . . . live . . ." he moaned, a weak smile on his face.

"I don't know about that," Tim said doubtfully. Jean kicked him.

"Here," Jack said, lurching over to Tumen. He gestured for him to hold out his hands. Into his right hand, he dropped the three metal gems: bronze, silver and gold. Into his left, he carefully placed the amulet, closing Tumen's fingers around it.

Tumen looked at Jack in gracious wonder.

But before anyone could say anything else, a crowd of Pirate Guards approached. The mining had stopped when the city transformed from silver back into its natural state, creating an upheaval. Upon seeing Jack and his friends there, they immediately drew swords and muskets.

"Oh, good," Jack said with humour. "That snake-thing in there was just a nice warm-up." He pulled his – or rather, Mr Reece's – sword.

But Captain Smith cleared her throat.

"Madame Minuit, Left-Foot and Silverback are no longer in charge here," she announced, as if it were the most casual thing in the world. "However, if you're looking for work aboard a *reputable* ship, I am interviewing for crew on the *Fleur de la Morte*."

"The *Fleur*?" A Pirate Guard whispered to another enthusiastically.

Jack looked at Arabella. She shrugged. Apparently her mother really *was* famous. Among pirates, at least.

No longer pursued by the Pirate Guards,

the crew of the *Barnacle* was escorted back to the docks. The guards – who were in awe of Captain Smith – even assisted Mr Reece back to the ship.

"It's the hat," Jack decided, wistfully looking at the fantastic plume in Captain Smith's velvet tricorn. "They all love the hat."

"Sure, Jack, it's the hat," Arabella said with a grin.

"You'll see, I'll get a hat like that for myself," Jack promised.

"Whatever you say, Captain Jack Sparrow," Tumen said with a smile.

Everyone gathered at the docks. The day had fully arrived, and soft yellow sunshine once again shone on New Orleans. Neither bronze, nor silver, nor gold – just brick and stone and wood. A living city.

A city that, if truth be told, smelled a little foul.

"It's so nice to see everything back to normal," Jean said, grinning at his home town. "I would rather have a bowl of alligator gumbo than whatever it is they eat in cities of gold any day!"

"I don't know about that," Captain Laura Smith and Jack said at the same time. They looked at each other a little guiltily. It would have been nice to have the gold – at least a little bit of it. Could come in handy someday.

"Well, that's it, then," Jack said, not one for long goodbyes. "All aboard who's going aboard the mighty *Barnacle*. Fare thee well, Cap'n Smith." He gave an exaggerated bow to Arabella's mother, complete with removing his hat and twirling it. Captain Smith gave a stiff little bow back. Their heads almost touched.

"Andihopeineverrunintoyouonthe-sevenseas," Jack muttered quickly.

"Foreverwillbetoolongifineverseeyou-again," Captain Smith agreed.

No one else appeared to have heard them.

Tim Hawk stretched his arms and smiled.

"Well . . . this has been fun, lads and lasses, and cats." Tim took a deep breath. "But I have got a family to find. After all, I was on my way to do that when Madame Minuit kidnapped me. Seems like a lost cause, I know, but Arabella thought *her* mother was dead for all those years – and here she is, alive. Maybe my mum and da' are still alive too, somewhere! There's a chance . . ."

"Of course, lad," Jack said with an understanding smile. Then he turned to Fitzwilliam and tapped his head as if to indicate Tim's insanity.

"There's always hope," Arabella said, slapping Jack around the back of his head.

"Take this." Tumen carefully handed Tim

the silver gem. Tim's eyes goggled in amazement. "Family is far more important than gold. I hope this brings you luck in finding them."

"And you'll always have my thanks for rescuing *us* from Madame Minuit's paralyzing snakes at the Masquerade Noir," Jack added. "Any time you need a favour, you just ask for old Jack Sparrow. I give you my word. And that's as good as anything else I can give you." Jack muttered the last part.

Tim nodded and grinned.

There were worse things than having an adventurous sea captain owe you a favour. He ran off, looking happier than the crew of the *Barnacle* had seen him since they'd met.

"All right, then, where were we?" Jack said, looking around. "Oh, yes – goodbye!"

He then threw his arm around Arabella's shoulders and started to head for the *Barnacle*.

But Arabella hesitated.

"What?" Jack asked, confused. "What's wrong now?"

Her lips were quivering. For the first time ever, she looked unsure of herself.

"Look, Jack, me and me mum, we sort of have to work . . . well . . ."

"You want to *stay* with her?" Jack said flatly. Captain Smith looked surprised.

Arabella shrugged plaintively. "I want to give her a chance at least. D'ye understand? I've never felt so free as I have with you on the *Barnacle*. I've never had such adventures . . . or *friends* before. And I feel so bad, especially after ye made me yer first mate and all . . ." She smiled at Jack for a moment, then squared her shoulders in determination. "But I've missed her so much . . . I don't want to lose her again. I'm going to stay with her and Mr Reece on the *Fleur de la Morte*."

"Forever?" Jack asked.

"For now," Arabella responded.

A shadow of emotion flickered over Jack's face. "Well, do what you have to, love," he said softly. Then he shook himself and gave a fierce smile. "We're all free to come and go on the *Barnacle*. That's the point, is it not? We're all free to do as we please! Good luck with that, Bell!"

Jack noticed Arabella's eyes grow watery.

"You're crying, lass."

"Just something in me eye," Arabella said, throwing her arms around Jack's neck. "Thank ye for everything, Jack," she sobbed. "Ye really are the best mate I've ever had – ever *will* have."

Arabella wiped her eyes and then hugged Fitzwilliam. The normally stiff aristocrat was blinking hard and trying to keep his face composed, but tears were running uncontrollably down his cheeks.

"Ye gods," Jack muttered. He nudged the boy. "Steady on there, Fitzy."

"I am *not* crying," Fitzwilliam insisted.

Arabella smiled sadly and gave him her kerchief to wipe his face with. It looked like an old cleaning rag, but Fitzwilliam took it with delight, as if it were made of French lace.

"All. Right. Then," Jack said, taking a deep breath. Arabella went to stand between her mother and Mr Reece, trying to look brave. "Everyone. *Else*. Aboard. The *Barnacle*. Now." He made impatient gestures at Tumen and Jean. And even Constance.

"Actually, we will not be returning with you, either," Tumen said quietly. He spread his hands, showing the amulet. "I am going home now, and there is no need for you to travel to the Yucatan just to take me there. Captain Smith is headed down the Mayan coast to . . . *escort* a sugar shipment slightly out of its way."

Jack rolled his eyes and shook his head.

Tumen continued, grinning. "Now that I have the amulet to return, my village will take me back and reward me greatly when I tell them the tale of how I got it back in the first place. They'll be singing my story for many generations!"

"*Oui*, and I and Constance will be joining him in the good life," Jean added, giving his sister a scratch under the chin. "We had a fantastic time on this *voyage*, Jack, but adventuring is *très dangereuse* business. We are retiring early, my sister and I. *Very* early. We are going to live in Tumen's village and fish for the rest of our days. Eh, *mon petit?*"

Constance purred in agreement, no doubt envisioning plentiful fish heads for years to come. She hissed a little at Jack. But only a little.

"Well, off you go, then," Jack said cheerfully, strangely unconcerned that he had just lost most of his crew. He turned to Fitzwilliam. "Please tell me that *you're* not coming with me either."

Fitzwilliam tried to hide a smile. "I am afraid I have nowhere else to go, Jack."

"That's *Captain*," Jack corrected. "On you go, then, I *guess*." he added grudgingly.

Fitzwilliam stepped aboard, followed by Jack, who took the tie line with him. Jack made himself very busy coiling the lines, but watched as everyone else stepped on to the *Fleur de la Morte*, each disappearing before he or she boarded the invisible ship. Arabella turned around and waved. Then she took a step into what looked like thin air and vanished.

Epilogue

The sun shone brightly over a calm, aquamarine sea. Puffy little storybook clouds drifted across the sky. Occasionally, a gull cried and a silver fish jumped out of the water. A good breeze kept the air from getting too hot and filled the sails of the *Barnacle*. Perfect sailing weather.

Jack and Fitzwilliam sat listlessly on deck. Jack was tossing little pebbles into a coil of rope and Fitzwilliam was looking at Arabella's kerchief.

The waves made little lapping noises against the side of the boat.

"Well, this is dead boring," Jack finally said, breaking the silence. "Who would have ever thought it would just be you and me aboard this vessel? How *very* ironic, as you were the only member of my not-so-faithful crew that I tried to keep *off* the ship."

They lapsed into silence again. Jack drew his cutlass and watched its golden tip glint in the sun.

"Well. What now?" Fitzwilliam asked, after a very long, very awkward silence. He put Arabella's kerchief in his breast pocket, stood up and stretched.

For once, Captain Jack Sparrow had no answer. Fitzwilliam moved over to the broadside of the ship and pulled out his pocket watch. He smiled as it glowed warmly in the sun. He was happy to have it back. It was the last connection he had to his long- lost sister.

Jack also got up and joined Fitzwilliam – for now, the only source of amusement on the *Barnacle*. He grabbed the gold watch and turned it over in his hands, trying to see what was so special about it.

"You're an overly sentimental fool, Fitzy. What's so special about this highfalutin, aristocratic trinket of yours?"

Fitzwilliam's nostrils flared, and his eyes flashed with anger. "Give it back!"

Suddenly, the perfectly clear blue sky grew dark with scudding clouds. Rolling thunder echoed over the sea.

"At ease, there, Fitzy. Here, take it," Jack said quickly, clapping the watch back into Fitzwilliam's hand. He looked at the sky, spooked. It didn't seem like a coincidence that the angry aristocrat's temper had flared up along with this from-out-of-nowhere storm. They had, after all, encountered a pirate named Captain Torrents who could stir storms with his anger.*

"That was *not* me," Fitzwilliam said, pointing out over the sea. "Look!"

A huge ship emerged from below the waves and came at them quickly. It was covered from stem to stern in human bones. Jack didn't need to see it up close to know whose ship this was. It was famous in nightmares and horror stories across the Seven Seas.

"The *Flying Dutchman*," he said, his voice thick with dread.

But before Fitzwilliam could ask what that meant, a bolt of lightning flashed. A figure appeared on deck beside them as if it had always been there, just waiting for the right moment to make itself seen. He was huge and his tentacled face squirmed in the

*In our very first volume, *The Coming Storm*

shadows. His voice cracked with evil.

"Boy," he growled at Fitzwilliam, "best give me yer watch or suffer the consequences at my hands. The hands of the Captain of the *Flying Dutchman*. The hands of *Davy Jones!*"

To be continued!

Don't miss the next volume in the continuing adventures of Jack Sparrow and the crew of the mighty <u>Barnacle</u>!

The Timekeeper

Jack has lost all of his crew to the *Fleur de la Morte* . . . except for Fitzwilliam P. Dalton III. Now, Jack and Fitz must face the greatest danger of the Seven Seas – the feared Davy Jones – all on their own. Don't miss our next volume, or you'll be very, very sorry you did. Savvy?